LANCASTER COUNTY SECOND CHANCES

RUTH PRICE

TABLE OF CONTENTS

ACKNOWLEDGMENTS

All Praise first to the Almighty God who has given me this wonderful opportunity to share my words and stories with the world. Next, I have to thank my family, especially my husband Harold who supports me even when I am being extremely crabby. Further, I have to thank my wonderful friends and associates with Global Grafx Press who support me in every way as a writer. Lastly, I wouldn't be able to do any of this without you, my readers. I hold you in my heart and prayers and hope that you enjoy my books.

All the best and Blessings,

Ruth.

CHAPTER ONE

Katie Olsen looked out the kitchen window. The sun was just coming up, and everyone but her *mamm* and younger sister were already out in the fields. It was spring, and the rising sun spread its beams over soft brown earth, ready for planting. The landscape was the same as she remembered. The gentle hills of her Lancaster County home seemed to be forever rolling away to the horizon. It had always been a comforting view.

She picked at the white cotton tablecloth with her fingers. It was the same familiar table cloth she had used as a child – the hand sewn border, the faint stain from the strawberry accident, the little uneven nubs that she had loved to rub with her fingers.

This plain white farmhouse still looked just the same as it had when she was six years old. The massive gray barn had seemed endless then, and it still looked huge. The freshly-tilled earth would soon be filled with movement and color and sound.

This farm had been her home. She had felt so comfortable in it, as if she herself had been a young plant springing up from her *daed*'s fields. She had grown from this soil, like the oak trees overshadowing the house. Like her mamm's roses. Like the wheat that swayed and whispered secrets to the lavender twilight. Once, her world had been as safe and predictable as bud and bloom and harvest. It had seemed to her that nothing would ever change.

But everything had changed. She was 26 now. The familiar white farmhouse wasn't her home any longer. It was her parents' home.

The tablecloth, the house, the barn, the oak trees, and even the rolling hills, all of them belonged to the child she had been, not the young woman she had become.

For the past three months, she had been an increasingly uncomfortable guest in her parents' home.

Maybe even a burden.

Of course, her mamm and daed would never put it that way. And she did her best to help them around the house and with her little sister and brother.

But still.

Katie's fingertip raised the corner of a paper lying underneath her breakfast plate. Her mamm had "forgotten" it there this morning.

It was an Amish advertising circular. The headline read: Young Widowed Men Interested in Remarriage.

A cheerful voice interrupted Katie's thoughts.

"Why such a sad face, Katze?"

Katie pulled her lips into a smile and turned to face her 10-year-old sister, Bett.

"No sad face for you, Bett." She pulled her blonde giggle box of a sister into her arms and smiled. "Come, I will help you with your chores."

They walked out to the chicken coop and roused the hens. Katie had always liked gathering eggs – the sleepy, blinking hens, the feel of their soft feathers, the warm, smooth eggs.

Bett was skipping in her joy. "I'm glad you're back, Katze," she was saying, calling Katie by the nickname everyone in her family used. Bett's blue eyes were full of affection.

Katie stopped gathering eggs momentarily. She bit her lip. She wished she could say, I am glad to be back, but that would have been a lie, and she already had too many sins on her soul.

"I'm glad you are pleased," was what she said.

"Everyone is pleased," Bett nattered on. "Last Sunday I

heard Mr. Hershberger say that you have a pleasing countenance and that you are a diligent worker. And Mr. Beiler said that he's glad you're back, and that it's a good thing."

Bett dug a toe into the dirt and smiled shyly up at Katie.

"I think they like you," she added, in a conspiratorial tone.

Katie stifled an impatient exclamation. Mr. Hershberger was 20 years her elder. He was bald and fat and had an ungovernable temper. And Mr. Beiler was 70 if he was a day and as shriveled as a stick. The last thing in the world she wanted was to attract the attention of men like Mr. Hershberger and Mr. Beiler.

Or, really, the attention of any man.

She closed her eyes and counted slowly to ten before saying, "I think that's all for now, Bett. Let's take these back."

Bett giggled and skipped along beside her. "I can't wait until I'm your age, Katze," she confided, "and all the men are asking after me."

Katie said nothing in reply, but she was wishing with all her soul that she could somehow revert to her sister's age and once again be a freckled, laughing child.

**

At dinner that night, the table was laden with baked bread and butter, beans and bacon, ham, baked potatoes, apple pie topped with cheese. It was good, solid farmhouse cooking, some of which Katie had made herself, but she had no appetite.

Katie's mamm shot her husband a glance. He straightened in his chair and cleared his throat.

"Are you feeling ill, Katze?" he rumbled.

"No, Daed," she replied.

"Eat, then."

She dutifully picked up a forkful of potatoes and put it into her mouth.

Katie retreated to bed immediately after dinner, pleading a throbbing head. Her parents had put her in her old bedroom. It still looked much the same as it had – the bare wooden floor, the plain single bed next to the big window overlooking the fields, the same starburst quilt that her grandmother had made for her when she born, with its red, blue, and green.

Even her old toys were still there – the old cotton doll and the stuffed bear that she had worn to shreds, all still lying at the bottom of the quilt chest at the foot of her bed.

There was the prayer book she had used as a child, still with her childish scrawls inside.

The old bedroom should have been a reassuring haven, but

for Katie, it was oddly jarring – a reminder of what she wasn't anymore, and could never be again.

Just as she had always done, she knelt down beside the bed for her evening prayers. As a child, it had been easy and natural for her to pray to God. She had felt His presence everywhere. But tonight, she found no words to say. Now, she didn't feel His presence at all.

She had not felt His presence for months. Sometimes, in her darkest moments, she even feared that God had…

The sound of a soft knock at Katie's bedroom door ended her devotions. Katie rose and opened the door to find her mamm standing outside. The candlelight touched her braided brown hair with gold.

"May I come in?"

"Of course." Katie sat down on the bed and patted the space beside her. Katie's mamm sat down quickly and put an arm around her. Her eyes looked worried.

"I shouldn't have left that advertisement on the table. I think I've upset you," she said softly. "I'm sorry. I didn't mean to."

"You have a right," Katie replied, looking down.

"It's not about our rights," her mamm corrected quickly. "Your daed and I, we just want to see you smile again. To come back again, just a little bit." She smoothed a tendril of

Katie's soft brown hair back from her face. "It was too soon, maybe."

"You're not the only ones," Katie told her, with an unhappy grimace. "Bett told me today that Mr. Hershberger and Mr. Beiler were asking after me," Katie added, wrinkling her nose.

Her mamm burst out laughing and hugged her close. "Then I don't blame you for picking at your food tonight." She smiled. "It would trouble me, too."

Katie smiled in spite of herself, and her mamm laughed again. "There," she said tenderly, lifting Katie's chin. "That's what I was looking for. My Katze."

Suddenly everything that had happened, everything that she had lost, welled up in Katie's heart. "Oh, Mamm!" she cried, and sobbed as her mamm made soothing noises and rocked her back and forth like a child.

CHAPTER TWO

The next morning, Katie was up long before dawn and long before anyone else was awake. She dressed by the light of a single candle and went down to the empty kitchen. She put a piece of cheese between two slices of bread, wrapped it in a handkerchief, and put it in a bag.

She started a fire in the fireplace to make the house warm, put on her own coat, and went outside.

The predawn dark was still very damp and cold. A thick fog covered everything. Karl, her daed's old collie, was curled up in a box on the porch. He opened one eye and mustered a few thumps of his tail in greeting.

Katie bent down and ruffled his fur, then walked to the barn. Her old blue bicycle was still in the corner. She walked it out into the yard, adjusted the bag around the handlebars, and pushed off into the fog.

The beautiful pastures of Lancaster County slowly rolled past. At first, in the dark, she knew them by the sweet smell of freshly-turned earth, the faint sound of dogs barking far away, the lowing of a cow. Then the sky began to lighten, and the fog faded to reveal big, rolling hills, which, though dark brown now, would soon be alive with fresh green. Katie inhaled deeply. She loved the scent of freshly turned earth, of dew, of new things stirring in the grass.

She pedaled past the Iverson farm, the Johansen farm, the Muller farm. Each field conjured up faces and names from the past. Most of the boys had been blonde, gangly, and tall. A few had hinted that they might like to court with her. She almost smiled, remembering John Muller and his shy calf eyes.

Of course, they hadn't ended up together. She had left home five years ago and her parents told her that John hadn't shown interest in anyone else for a good two years. That is, until Laura Pedersen grew up and caught his eye.

A sudden pain in her shoulder made Katie grimace and slow her pace.

When she was Bett's age, Katie could have arrived in town within 30 minutes. But it was becoming clear that this time, it would take her twice that, if not longer. It wasn't the fog that hindered her – she knew every pebble in those well-worn roads. She could have ridden them with her eyes closed.

It was her shoulder. The damp made it ache, and she had to go slowly to avoid pulling it. Her bandages had only come off a week before, and she couldn't bear the thought of facing another doctor.

She closed her eyes and let the bicycle bounce freely down a long, straight slope. She tried to shut it out, but even this small reminder made her peaceful thoughts drift away like the morning mists.

It made the doctor's face come back again, as it had been coming back every day for the last three months.

"I'm sorry," he was saying, and put a hand on her arm. "Is there anything you'd like us to do?"

She heard herself screaming, *Gott im Himmel*!

She put a hand to her mouth, and momentarily the handlebars left her control. The bicycle bounced dangerously off a rock and she had to hit the brakes to keep the bicycle from crashing.

Gott…

The bicycle skidded to a stop, and Katie dug her heels into the gravel to keep herself from falling over. She could feel herself trembling. She tried again to pray, to plead, to feel something, but there was nothing.

Maybe she should never have left. Maybe God had meant her to stay here, to marry John Muller.

She must not have done God's will. Because surely, if she had done it, her life wouldn't have gone so horribly wrong.

God must be angry with her, so terribly…

Katie closed her eyes and stood very still, feeling the muffled pounding of her heart. Minutes passed. A door closed somewhere in the distance, a man's voice issued a short, sharp command, and a dog barked.

God did not strike her dead. The world did not end.

She put a hand to her eyes and pushed off again.

***

"Guten morgen, Katie!"

It wasn't hard for Katie to muster a smile for Elie Meissen. Elie's face was as plump and red as a ripe apple, and it was always smiling. Katie had never seen her in a bad mood, but if Elie had a fault, it was that she had the longest tongue in three counties. Elie loved to get news, and she loved even more to report it.

"Guten morgen, Elie Meissen."

The Meissens ran a store in town and made their living

mainly off of the sale of quilts, furniture, and other handmade crafts to tourists.

Elie tilted her head to one side, like a bird. "What brings you to town, Katie?"

"I'm looking for a job," Katie replied. "I need work, and was wondering who might need help."

Elie's bright eyes sparkled with this new intelligence. "Ah! I wish we could help you, but we already have three women who make quilts." She put a finger to her lips. "Maybe I can ask around for you."

She waved Katie around to the back of the counter. "So you came on your bicycle? That's a fair way from your farm. Have you had your breakfast?"

Katie shrugged. "I have bread and cheese."

"Bah," Elie laughed. "Come back to the office and have pie and coffee."

Elie led the way to a small office with one wooden table and three chairs. There was a small counter on one wall, and it was covered with kitchen clutter. Elie pulled out a chair for Katie and poured a cup of steaming hot coffee. "Take a piece of pie. It's coconut cream from last night. So good." Elie put a plate on the table and licked her thumb.

Katie didn't feel especially hungry, but took a few bites to be polite. The pie was very good – rich and creamy and indulgent.

"I'm so glad you're back," Elie confided, pulling up a chair. "So much has happened since you left. Let me catch you up."

Katie stifled a sigh and braced herself. Elie was never happy until she had told all she knew. Or thought she knew.

"Terese Johansen spent *rumspringa* in Philadelphia running wild with the English, they say. She has decided to leave altogether and become a Presbyterian. Her parents are prostrated, I can tell you."

Katie was tempted to offer a tentative rebuke for Elie's gossip, but thought better of it. She was grateful that Elie was sharing news rather than asking painful questions.

Katie's annoyance softened. She was also sure that Elie's unusual forbearance was not accidental. Given Elie's love of gossip, her restraint on that point was an act of grace. Katie sipped her coffee and said nothing.

"And did you know that Martin Hoffer is the new bishop after old David Zurich died? Remember how we almost used to go to sleep during services?" She giggled. "Well, not anymore! No one can have any peace during his sermons, let alone sleep! He's the strictest bishop anyone can remember. So stern!" Her cheerful face grew scrunched up momentarily as she took a sip of coffee. "It gives me heartburn."

Katie's conscience stirred again, and again she squelched

it.

"Oh!" Elie fanned her face. "And there's another newcomer besides you! Of course, you're not new, and he is, but you know what I mean. It's a widower with four *kinner*, a man named Joseph Lapp. He's from the next county. Quite good looking, so I hear. Tall. A little peaked, though."

Katie stirred uncomfortably, and Elie nattered on. "Of course, every woman in the county who has a grown daughter has set her cap for him. Though he's a little old for a girl."

A sudden ringing from the shop announced the arrival of a customer. Katie breathed a sigh of relief as Elie jumped up and finally tended to her own business.

Or almost tended to it. She could just hear the sound of a woman's voice and Elie's voice in reply. After the initial greetings, their voices lowered, but not before Katie heard the words, "Oh, the poor thing."

She sighed, shook out her skirt, and rose to leave.

CHAPTER THREE

That evening after dinner Katie went to bed early again. She undressed by the light of a candle, peeling off the plain blue dress and black stockings. She stood in front of the mirror. The sad young woman who looked back at her had soft, wavy brown hair, large, earnest green eyes, and a body that her mamm had once told her was "womanly."

Except for the stain. And now, the scar.

It was vain, and wrong, but she couldn't resist running her finger over the scar on her shoulder. Her skin was still tender from the surgery. The angry red color had faded, and the doctor had promised that it would continue to fade until it could hardly be seen. But at three months out, a faint splotch was still there, still visible, though barely, in the dim light.

The stain had been the size of a dinner plate. Its outline had been ragged and ugly. It had looked as if her right shoulder had been splashed with red wine. The purple birthmark had been her secret shame, and also her secret vanity. It had covered three inches of her upper arm, the right side of her neck, and two inches of her back.

She had hated it all her life, but her parents had told her that God loved her, and that they loved her, and that it made no difference – that it was vain to be concerned about things that did not endanger her health.

But in her vanity, she had chosen to have the hated mark removed anyway.

Katie knelt by the bed and clasped her hands. She tried to pray the prayers she had learned as a child, to be pious and meek, but something in her convulsed, and her grief suddenly came spilling out.

Oh, God, was it this? Was this why? So much, only for this?

Why not me, then?

The only reply was the sound of the candle sizzling as it wept its small tears. Katie searched her heart for any answer, any sense of God's nearness, any comfort.

Oh, God, where are you?

There was no sound, no spark of feeling. Nothing.

Sobs welled up in her throat, and her head drooped over the bed. She stopped trying to pray. It was useless. And she was too tired to spend another night with her hands over her face. She rose, blew out the candle, and slipped under the covers.

Katie was exhausted, and sleep came quickly. She felt as if her body was falling into some measureless depth, down into some infinity of sleep. Waves of unconsciousness closed over her, pushing her further and further down.

"Katze."

She turned her head and murmured softly.

"Katze."

The curtain rolled back, and she was in her own bedroom again, under the eiderdown blanket. Erik was there with her, and she smiled and rolled to face him.

His hands smoothed over her shoulders. "You are good to hold," he whispered and kissed her neck. "You are smooth."

He kissed her neck again.

"You are round."

His hands glided over her shoulders and moved down.

"You fill my hands like apples warmed by the sun."

Erik's hands moved back over her right shoulder – paused – and lingered.

Her smile faded. She pulled back slightly.

His hands stopped moving. His brown eyes were suddenly serious.

"Why will you not let me touch you?"

She turned her face into the pillow. "Because I am ashamed."

He turned her face to his again. "Ashamed? Of this? It's nothing."

"It's ugly. It makes me feel as if I am ugly, too."

He put his lips to her hair. "You know that I love you?" he whispered.

She nodded. "I know."

"Would I lie to you?"

She shook her head.

"Then believe me when I tell you that you are beautiful."

"How can you say such a thing, when I wear such an ugly mark?" she had murmured. "It's like a burn."

He had sighed, and rested his cheek against hers, as if he despaired of her reason. "Katie Olsen, I am your husband, you have borne me a son, and yet never once have you let my hand rest on your shoulder. This idea of yours is unhealthy."

"I can't help it," she had whispered, turning her face into the pillow again.

He had sighed again, deeply, and had been silent for a long while. Then, "Look at me."

She had looked up into his eyes. They were warm and tender.

"This thing makes no difference to me. But it makes a difference to you. It isn't good or healthy for a woman like you to feel ugly. This thing makes you shy with me, and that is not good." He paused again and added, "Maybe we should go to the doctor and have it removed."

She had turned to face him. "Erik, really? But wouldn't that be wrong? Wouldn't it be vanity, a sin?"

He was silent again. He finally said, "It is more wrong for this to come between us than it could ever be to go to the doctor."

"Oh, Erik, I don't know whether to be glad or sorry," she had cried.

"Be glad," he had said, and kissed her. His lips were warm and sweet, juicy as a just-ripe tomato.

Katie stirred in her sleep, turned. Erik's kiss faded into the velvet dark. Somewhere, maybe in her dream or maybe outside of it, raindrops hit the window. She pushed a bare foot beyond the warmth of the covers.

The dream shifted. Now she was in her garden picking tomatoes. It was deep summer, and the garden was head-high with green leaves. Peder was there with her, holding a basket. His dark curls were swallowed up by a straw hat that was many times too big for him. He was three years old, only just big enough to walk, in his little shirt and trousers.

He was singing in his high childish voice, a silly nonsense song about the goat who tried to float, the calf that only laughed, and the word the bird heard.

"Where did you learn such a song, silly Peder?" she teased him. "You're too big to believe that a goat can float."

He had smiled at her from beneath the hat. Only his pink mouth had been visible.

"I learned it from the Bible," he had said stoutly.

"From the Bible?"

"Yes. In the Bible, it says that all the animals went into the ark. Goats and calves and birds."

"Yes, but – "

"Well, the goats in the ark floated. The dove heard God say, 'Go back to the ark.' And if you were a calf that day, wouldn't you laugh?"

She had dropped the tomatoes. Then she had turned on her

astonished son and chased him up and down the garden until she caught him.

"Mamm, Mamm!" Peder's squeals of delight were so shrill that they pulled her up from the depths of sleep. She sighed and opened her eyes. Peder ran away, and his fading laughter dissolved into a familiar call.

It was just sunrise, and a rooster in the yard below was crowing.

CHAPTER FOUR

Joseph Lapp sat perfectly silent, ramrod-straight, and with his eyes facing front. He was at church and trying hard to be inconspicuous.

Even though that was nearly impossible. He was six foot three and had four kinner. His three small sons and preteen daughter stretched out to his right like beads on a necklace.

It was his custom to sit on the back row at church meetings. It was a coping strategy he had learned early. Emma was a quiet girl, but the boys had more than once required him to make a hasty exit. Caleb, his youngest, still wanted to whisper during meeting.

"Daed," Caleb hissed, leaning close. His upturned eyes were like blue marbles, but Joseph had learned that this innocent expression usually preceded mischief. Joseph looked down at him, thinking that it might be time for a warning pinch.

Although, to be fair, the bishop had kept them for more than two hours, which was a long time for a five-year-old boy to be still.

He turned slightly, scoping out the rear of Mr. Fisher's barn in case a hasty exit became necessary. There were only two elders between him and the door, though some of the other churchgoers might be disturbed if he had to take Caleb out.

He glanced over at the opposite row, where the women sat. There were only three women in the back row: an older woman who must have been John Fisher's wife, a young woman, and a little girl.

The younger woman was on the end of the row, and held his attention momentarily. He couldn't help noticing that she was very pretty, but that wasn't the most noticeable thing about her. All the other women, and even the girls, maintained an expression of grave piety, but this woman's face was as expressive of misery as an audible moan. Her eyes were large and filled with sadness. Her lower lip drooped like a child's.

The sound of his son's voice snapped Joseph back to

himself. "Daed," Caleb hissed again, "I have to pee!"

Joseph turned to his son, searched his face, and thought it more likely that Caleb was bored. He leaned in.

"Can you hold it?"

The little boy shook his head vehemently, but smiled – a sure sign that he was faking. Joseph pinched his lips in exasperation.

"Try to hold it. The service is almost over." He settled in his chair and tried to focus on the sermon. "Settle down."

He refocused his attention on the service. The new bishop, Martin Hoffer, had been chosen to deliver the message that morning. He was preaching an unusually strong sermon against the sins of pride and arrogance.

The older man's dark eyes were stern and looked disapproving. His mouth was pinched into a thin, straight line.

Joseph glanced over at his kinner's bobbing hats, hoping that they were not getting the idea that God was angry or harsh. It would have been an easy mistake. Martin Hoffer tended to be strict, and his words were perhaps too strong for kinner still tender from the loss of their mamm.

Maybe he should take Caleb outside, after all.

"Our God is a holy God," the new bishop was saying, "a God of lightning and thunder! A God of roaring seas and earthquakes! A God who does not tolerate rebellion!"

Joseph glanced back toward the door again. The two elders had disappeared.

"Our God is a holy God. A God who hates the arrogance of the vain and proud!"

There was a strangled gasp, and Joseph turned to check his kinner. To his relief, they were sober as little judges. The sound had come from elsewhere.

To Joseph's astonishment, the young woman across the way now looked not just sad, but positively ill. The older woman, who he guessed to be her mamm, was whispering anxiously in her ear. The girl shook her head and leaned back into the chair with her eyes closed, as if she felt faint.

The bishop scanned his audience with narrowed eyes. "Seeing that these things are true, then, let us serve God acceptably with reverence and godly fear, as the Scriptures say.

"For our God is a consuming fire!"

With shocking suddenness, the young woman leapt up and bolted out through the door like a frightened deer. Her mamm turned and followed almost at a run.

The noise and movement turned a few heads, but the bishop preached on, undeterred. No one gave any further sign of having noticed anything.

Joseph noticed with alarm that his kinner's hats were beginning to bob. The boys craned their necks toward the back door, whispering to one another.

"Hush," Joseph told them. "Be quiet!"

But he himself could hardly help wondering what had just happened, and why.

After the service the church members gathered on the lawn for lunch. Tables and chairs were laid out and ready, and the congregants sat down to eat. Joseph noticed that Mrs. Fisher reappeared to help serve the meal, and that the girl helped. But the young woman who had fled so abruptly did not return.

Daniel Gruber, sitting at his elbow, asked him if he would stay on his own farm, or if he planned to work for the English. Joseph coughed into his hand.

"I will be making furniture for an English cabinet maker in town," he replied. "It's not convenient, because I have to hire an English driver to take me back and forth to work, but it will not be forever. I will only be working there until I can sell my old farm and buy a new farm in Lancaster County. I plan to move my family here."

Daniel Gruber nodded and said nothing, and Joseph did not elaborate. Everyone in his new church knew why he and his kinner needed the change. Their own home had become a place of sadness and loss, and a change of scene would be good for the kinner.

Perhaps for him, also.

"The only thing that troubles me," Joseph explained, "is that I need someone to help with my kinner. My daughter is trying hard, but she is only 12, and I cannot be there to help her while I work. Do you know of such a person? I might hire an English helper, but I would rather hire an Amish one."

Daniel Gruber munched a biscuit. "Young Katie Olsen, John Fisher's daughter, is looking for a job, they say," he replied, after a heavy silence.

"John Fisher's daughter?" he asked in surprise, though he did not add, the one who just ran out of the service?

Daniel Gruber nodded. "Yes. She came back to her parents three months ago." He paused again and added, "She was married to Erik Olsen. A good man."

"I remember him," Joseph replied. "I met him when we were younger. He is a good man. I'm sorry to hear of his troubles."

Daniel looked up in surprise. "You didn't hear about the accident?"

Joseph shook his head.

"Erik died three months ago. And his little boy."

Seeing that Joseph had been struck speechless, Daniel

continued, "There was a fire at the house." He glanced around for Mrs. Fisher, and when he didn't see her nearby, added in a low voice, "It was very sad. Lightning struck a big tree near the house. It crashed through the roof and fell on the little boy's bed. He was trapped under it. Erik couldn't get him out and wouldn't leave him. Of course, their neighbors came when they saw the fire, but by the time they came, they could not get in for the flames. In spite of all they could do, the house burned to the ground, with both man and boy inside."

"*Auch das noch!*"

"Katie was away in the hospital that night, or she would most likely have died in the same way. It has been very hard for her. She has only just begun to go out, to go to church again. But she is very changed."

Joseph fell into a stricken silence. He had never seen Katie before that day, but he remembered Erik Olsen. Once when they were both teens they had played on opposing baseball teams in a tournament. He had been the pitcher for his team, and Erik the best batter for their opponent's. In those days Joseph had thought himself an athlete, but Erik had taught him a lesson in humility. He had cracked one of Joseph's fastballs so far out in the corn that no one ever found it, not even when winter came and the land went flat and bare. Erik had been a fine, strong fellow with a ready laugh. A good sport.

Joseph shook his head and said no more, nor did Daniel

Gruber. But now Katie Olsen's strange behavior made perfect sense to Joseph. Too much sense.

In fact, her sad eyes haunted him all during the long car ride back home, in spite of the fact that Caleb nattered and giggled and pulled on his sleeve the whole time.

CHAPTER FIVE

The next day Joseph paid the driver and walked into his house wearily, glad that the work day was over. His was a large, plain farmhouse, and it had once been comfortable. But after Sarah's death, the responsibility of running an Amish household had proven too heavy for their poor daughter, Emma.

She greeted him at the doorway, her pretty, heart-shaped face turned up to greet him. "Hello, Daed."

She was carrying a laundry basket filled with clothes.

He leaned down to kiss her, feeling a pang of guilt. Emma was too young to be burdened with the house and the boys and the cooking. She needed to concentrate on her schoolwork.

But most of all, she needed a woman to guide her.

He watched her anxiously as she skipped out the side door

to the clothes line. She was 12, poised like a chick on the edge of flight. Soon she would surge past this gangly stage of all arms and legs.

She was on the cusp of becoming a young woman, and he was not ready for that change.

The door swung open with her, and through the opening Joseph could see his sons working in the garden outside.

Hezekiah and Jeremy were old enough to do many things for themselves, but Caleb was only five and constantly getting into trouble. Joseph bit his lip, begrudging every day spent away from them, from the education they should be getting at this crucial time. He longed to be with his kinner every day, but until he could sell this farm, he had to work.

What he needed, and very badly, was a woman to help with the kinner while the farm was on the market.

He sat down in a kitchen chair and placed his hat on the table. He had been putting that task off for a while now, partly because there were so many other things to do, and partly because he couldn't stand the thought of another woman in Sarah's house.

He closed his eyes. The very thought of it seemed a violation. Sometimes it was hard for him to even believe that she was gone. He half-expected to hear the sound of her humming from the garden, or to catch a whiff of her apple jam cooking in the kitchen.

It was only last winter that she…

He stopped himself. He had been down that dark hall too many times. He had to make himself move forward, for his own sanity and for the sake of the kinner.

His thoughts returned to Katie Olsen. She was young enough to be strong, and old enough to be capable. He felt empathy for her grief and would like to help her, if he could.

But the look he had seen on her face that Sunday made him question whether she was ready to be with kinner, when she had just lost her own young son.

Maybe the arrangement wouldn't work out. Maybe it would do harm instead of good.

And in any case, he needed someone who was stable and responsible. What if she had another meltdown in front of his kinner? They had already had enough to upset them.

He sighed and put his hands up in a brief gesture of helplessness. "*Gott, hilf mir*," he prayed.

"Daed, Daed!" Jeremy called from outside. "What good does it do to plant these beans? Emma will make them taste like an old shoe!"

"I will not!" Emma cried, stung.

"We'll have to sell them to the English. Or maybe go to an English restaurant!"

"Oh!"

Joseph rose wearily and went outside.

By the next Sunday, Joseph was tired enough to risk taking a chance on the young woman. He still didn't like the idea of bringing a stranger into their home, but there was no other choice.

He arrived for worship with all his kinner in tow. The services were being held at Johan Carver's farm. The Carver farm was very pretty. It was a warm spring day, and there were close to a hundred people milling about. If he had not been on a mission, Joseph would have enjoyed the day. But to his own annoyance, he was tense.

To begin with, there was no sign of Katie. He wondered if she had been so overcome by whatever had upset her that she had now withdrawn from public.

He entered the barn, where chairs had been set up, and sat down in the back row again with his kinner beside him. It was a good vantage point, because he would be able to see everyone as they passed by. He didn't want to seem to be looking for Katie, because he didn't want to create the impression that he was interested in her for anything other than help with his kinner.

But Katie did not appear.

Joseph suppressed a frown. Perhaps it would be better to speak to her daed, anyway. Mr. Fisher was a solid, sensible man, not given to speculation.

Joseph shifted uncomfortably in his chair. He wished devoutly that he could say the same of others. He had begun to notice that women of a certain age were taking notice of him. Yes, another one, a matron in the row ahead of his, turned her head, made eye contact, and smiled. He nodded once.

He had already been the object of some pointed comments, mostly from women with young daughters. These helpers had pointed out to him that it was not good for young kinner to be without a mamm.

He bit his lip in irritation. It was one of the things that made Katie Olsen an attractive possibility. It was clear that she, at least, would not give him unwanted problems in that area.

The barn began to fill up, and just before the service started, Mr. Fisher and his family arrived. Joseph noticed with a twinge of worry that Katie was not with them.

But at least her daed had come.

Joseph found it hard to concentrate on the message that morning. He couldn't stop wondering if it was wise to make a grieving mamm an offer to work with kinner.

But he also wondered what he would do if he couldn't find

someone to help with his kinner.

After the service, as was the custom, the worshippers gathered for a meal on the lawn. Joseph left his kinner at the table and went to search for Mr. Fisher. He soon found him.

"Good morning, Mr. Fisher."

Mr. Fisher patted him on the back. "Guten morgen, Joseph."

Joseph suddenly felt awkward. He stuttered, "I have a question to ask you, Mr. Fisher. I hear your daughter is looking for work, and I need someone to help with my kinner while I am away at work. Would your daughter be willing to work for me? It would only be for a few months, until I can sell my farm. I would pay more than the going rate and provide transportation."

Mr. Fisher's brown eyes expressed surprise, followed swiftly by uncertainty. "It's a kind offer, but I can't promise that she will agree. She is a diligent worker, of course, but the kinner...you understand. It is still very soon." He looked down suddenly, and wiped his nose.

"Yes of course, I understand," Joseph replied softly. The look of grief he had seen in the older man's face reminded him that Mr. Fisher had been a grandfather. Joseph cleared his throat. He suddenly felt clumsy.

"I will be at the next meeting," he continued. "If your daughter agrees to help me with my kinner, we will talk then."

"If she agrees, how will you arrange it so that you are not alone together?" Mr. Fisher asked.

Joseph nodded. "My English driver will take her to and from my house each day. I will be with her only in the car."

Mr. Fisher considered this, and finally grunted, "Very well. I will tell her."

"Thank you, Mr. Fisher."

Later that day, when Joseph had his little family back at home, he called them to the kitchen table.

"I want to talk with you about something," Joseph told them.

They sat down, suddenly serious. Joseph noticed with a pang that there was even a hint of fear in the eyes trained on him. He noticed that his oldest boy, Hezekiah, sat up straight, squared his shoulders, and put an arm around Caleb.

Joseph hastened to reassure them. "It's nothing bad. Something that I hope will be very good, for all of us." He took a deep breath and plunged in. "We have all had to pitch in and work harder lately. I have not been here to help, and I won't be able to help until we move. It isn't good for you kinner to be at home alone."

Emma suddenly saw what he was at. Her brown eyes widened, and she tried to cut him off.

"No, Daed!"

"Emma..."

"No!"

"Emma, it is unfair to you. To you, most of all."

"I can run the house. I can make it work. Just give me more time, and I will..."

The meaning was beginning to dawn on the boys. "You mean you want to bring someone here?" Hezekiah asked.

"Yes. I have invited a woman from Lancaster County to come and help us. She just lost her own little boy a few months ago, and she is very sad. It might help her to work, to be busy. And we need help with the house, a woman's help."

Caleb's lip trembled. "You mean instead of Mamm?" he cried.

"No," Joseph insisted, and held out his arms. Caleb rushed into them, and Joseph pulled him close. "No one could ever be instead of Mamm," he soothed. "This woman, she would be a helper only, just to cook and clean and help us with the house. Nothing more. Only until we get the new farm. She will understand this."

"I don't want a stranger in Mamm's house," Emma

protested. "Cooking in her kitchen, handling her things! We don't need another person. I can do it!"

"You have done a very good job," Joseph told her softly. "But you are not old enough yet to do all that needs to be done. If you were full grown, it would still be hard. No, we need a woman's help."

"I don't want a stranger in our house," Emma replied defiantly.

"It will not be for long," Joseph told her and was startled to hear the pleading tone in his own voice. He cleared his throat and took a new grip on the situation. "It may seem strange at first. But we need this woman's help. And she may need ours, for a while."

"What if she's mean?" Jeremy objected.

"She will not be unkind."

"What if she's ugly?" Caleb blurted, finger in mouth.

"She is not ugly. But you should not judge her by her looks, in any case. That is pride and vanity. You're old enough to know better, Caleb Lapp."

"It's a stranger in Mamm's house," Emma whimpered.

Joseph sensed that he didn't need to push the issue further, but concluded firmly, "I will say no more of it now."

The kinner knew this to be a sign that further argument

was useless, and fell silent. But Emma's eyes were smoldering, and the boys looked uncertain.

Joseph sighed and motioned for his kinner to come closer. "Let us pray," he murmured.

CHAPTER SIX

"Come out to the porch and swing a while, Katie," her daed said.

They had just finished a large dinner, and Katie had already prepared a big pan full of soapy water for the clean-up. But her mamm nodded and tilted her head toward the door, so Katie wiped her hands and followed her daed out into the soft spring twilight.

Her daed was a heavy man, and he sat down heavily on the porch swing. It jerked taut, and then swung out gently over the edge of the porch.

Katie smiled. This had been a nightly ritual during her

childhood. Every night, weather permitting, she had crawled up into this porch swing with her daed and poured out all her childish hopes and fears as he listened.

She sat down beside him and took his hand.

"I've missed this," she told him, leaning her head on his shoulder.

"So have I, Katze."

They rocked back and forth for a long while as the old chains squeaked and groaned. After the twilight had deepened to indigo, too dark to see a face, Katie's daed said, "I talked to Joseph Lapp today at meeting."

"Who is he?" Katie murmured.

"A man who lives in the next county. He asked about you."

"About me?" Katie stiffened, remembering her elderly admirers.

"Yes. He heard that you were looking for a job, and he says that he has one, if you're interested."

"Oh."

"His wife passed away last winter," her daed went on, "and he has three small boys and a girl. He wants to sell his farm and move to Lancaster County, but he is working for the English until he can sell. He needs a woman to look after his kinner. Only for a few months, he says."

Katie considered this news gravely.

"He has an English driver. He says he will be with you only in the car. I told him I would tell you." Katie's daed squeezed her hand. "You might pray about it?"

It would do no good, Katie thought, but only said, "No need, Daed. I will take the job."

"You don't have to," her daed added softly. "You can take your time. Choose whatever you like."

Katie stared out into the darkness. "I have to start sometime. It may as well be now."

"You are sure?"

"I'm sure."

"Well, it might be good. Work might help you. It has helped me. When I am sad, I find something to do," her daed replied, "something hard, like chopping wood or baling hay. I throw the sadness away with both my hands."

"Does it work, Daed?"

He kissed the top of her head. "Most often. And when it doesn't work, it makes me too tired to fret."

Katie smiled. "I love you, Daed."

"And I, you, little girl."

When the next Sunday came, Katie arrived at church feeling nervous. She smoothed her dress, trying to conceal her nerves. She had never met this Joseph Lapp or his kinner, and after the last painful service, she wasn't even looking forward to worship.

But she was still determined to accept the offer of work. Her parents had been gentle and patient, but Katie hated the thought of being a burden to them. They had enough to worry about.

She sat down with her family, fighting the impulse to scan the faces of newcomers. "What does he look like, this Joseph Lapp?" she whispered to her mamm.

Mary Fisher moved her eyes, but not her head. "There he is now."

Katie turned her head just enough to catch sight of a tall blonde man sitting in the back row. She could only see him in profile, since he was leaning over to whisper to a small brown-haired boy. Two older boys and a preteen girl filled the seats down the row.

Katie let her glance linger. Joseph Lapp was not unpleasant to look on. He was tall and fair, with very broad shoulders and a square jaw. His brows were bushy, his eyes were a startling blue, and his hair was straight and thick and blonde as summer wheat. He was clearly a powerful man, but as Elie's shrewd eye had noticed, he seemed worn by his recent loss.

A picture Katie had seen once flashed into her mind. When she was a child, she had once seen an old-fashioned engraving. It had been entitled Daniel and the Lions, and had depicted a huge golden lion with burning eyes and a tremendous mane.

Her mamm's voice hissed in her ear.

"Katze!"

Katie came to herself and cast her eyes down instantly.

But all during the service, Katie distracted herself from the sermon by wondering instead what sort of person Joseph Lapp would be and what his kinner were like. She dared not turn to look again, but she had seen that the youngest boy had straight brown hair, blue eyes, and a rosebud mouth.

Katie closed her eyes.

The service was shorter than usual that Sunday and was soon over. Katie didn't have to wonder if Joseph Lapp would be prompt with his offer, because not long after the service ended, she looked up and saw him standing by. He was shaking hands with her daed.

"Guten morgen, Mr. Fisher."

"Guten morgen, Joseph."

Katie's daed motioned to his family. "This is my wife, Mary, and my daughter, Katie."

Joseph Lapp extended a sun-browned hand to her mamm and then to Katie. Katie took it shyly. It swallowed hers and was very rough and strong. He trained his bright blue eyes on her face.

"My daed told me about your job," Katie ventured shyly.

"My offer stands, Katie. Would you like to take the job?"

Katie set her jaw. "Yes, I have decided. I will take the job."

"Good," Joseph replied briskly. "We can talk over lunch. You can meet my kinner. We will be glad to have the help." He raised his hands and laughed suddenly, and Katie caught a brief flash of white. "No, it is a relief. Thank you, Katie."

"You're welcome," Katie replied quietly. As the men turned to go, Katie's mamm shot her a quizzical look but said nothing.

Joseph invited the Fisher family to sit with his family for lunch. Katie sat down opposite the boys, who were openly curious.

"Well, you're not ugly, at any rate," Jeremy blurted, in a tone of relief.

"Jeremy!" Joseph barked, and Katie cracked a faint smile. The look of outraged mortification on her new employer's handsome face was almost funny.

"It's all right. I have younger brothers," she told him, and turned to Jeremy.

"How old are you?" she asked him.

"Seven. Eight next February."

"You're almost grown up, then."

Joseph recovered himself and did his best to move on. He put his hand on his oldest son's shoulder. "This is Hezekiah. You've met Jeremy, and this is my daughter, Emma."

"Hello, Hezekiah. It's nice to meet you," Katie nodded, and Hezekiah smiled. But Emma said nothing until her daed cleared his throat.

"Hello," she said, in a barely audible mumble.

Katie looked at Emma and was reminded of a calf – a gangly, awkward, adorable calf. Except that this calf was without its mamm. The lost look in her brown eyes went to Katie's heart. She mustered up a smile that she hoped looked more confident than it felt.

"I have a feeling you and I are going to be great friends," Katie told her.

"And this," Joseph added, "is my youngest, Caleb."

Caleb stared at her from the safety of his daed's lap. He had reverted to sucking his thumb, a sure sign of nervousness.

Katie looked at the child and was shocked by the strength of her feelings. One look at his pouting baby face and all her starving maternal instincts came surging back. She ached to hold the baby in her arms. It was all she could do to keep herself from reaching for him.

Her mouth formed a circle. "Oh….oh, what a fine little man," she said softly. "Hello, Caleb."

Caleb took his thumb out of his mouth and gave her a shy smile. Katie smiled back, and from that moment, and forever afterward, loved Caleb Lapp with all her heart.

She estimated that the other three kinner might take her a few seconds more.

CHAPTER SEVEN

The next morning just before sunrise, Katie was riding to the next county with Joseph and his English driver, a wizened elderly man named Eli Shandy. Mr. Shandy was brown and dry as a hickory nut, and about as communicative – a terse grunt was the only thanks she got for greeting him – but Joseph was warm and cordial and often half-turned to talk to her. Katie was relieved to find that Joseph was thoughtful of appearances and chose to sit in the passenger seat, leaving her the back seat.

Katie couldn't help thinking, though, that he had made a poor choice of conveyance, at least for himself. A sedan was simply too small for him. Joseph was very tall and very broad, and a good third of his back seemed to be sticking out beyond the seat. She could only imagine how cramped his legs must feel in that small car.

It was spring, and Amish kinner were not required to go to school in spring, since they were needed to help with the planting. Joseph was not planting a crop this year, but his kinner would nevertheless be needed at his farm.

"Emma will help you," he was saying, "and she will show you where everything is. If she sulks a little, don't mind her. She's a good girl; she'll come around.

"Hezekiah and Jeremy have their chores and won't be inside much except for lunch. Caleb will want to go outside with his brothers but should stay with you. His chore is to sweep the floor and take out the trash."

Katie listened carefully as he talked. He spent the most part of the drive giving her pointers about the kinner and the house and reviewing what needed to be done. Katie felt sympathy for him suddenly. His family had apparently gotten very much behind in their work. Joseph must have been beside himself without a woman in the house to keep things on track.

Katie wondered briefly what his wife had looked like. Had she been tall and strong, like him? Tiny and neat? Blonde? Brunette?

She felt her cheeks going warm at the thought, and checked herself. It was another sign of her terrible tendency to vanity, that she kept focusing on appearance instead of what was important – what was on the inside. She lowered her head. Joseph had no doubt chosen his wife based on what he saw in her spirit, not what he saw in her face. And it was none of her business, in any case.

Katie's mamm had told her that Mrs. Lapp had died the previous winter from influenza. It seemed such a sad way to die, Katie thought, and doubly so because it had been avoidable. Her mamm had said that Sarah Lapp had been too busy to listen to her body, until her sickness took over and she had to be rushed to the hospital. By that time, it was too late.

Joseph's brisk voice jolted her from her daydreams.

"Here we are."

Katie assessed her new place of employment. Joseph Lapp's farm was slightly larger than the average Amish farmhouse. It was a plain two-story clapboard house painted in a pale yellow. There were nice old elms in the yard, a big red barn, and a kitchen garden. Still, there was evidence of the family's recent upheaval. The lawn and garden looked decidedly scraggly, the mailbox was askew, and the porch was covered in what looked like feathers. Katie drew herself up. There was no telling what she would find inside the house, since after all, it had only been tended by a man and small kinner for the last six months.

The sound of the car driving up had attracted the Lapp kinner. They stood out on the front porch in the first rays of the sun, shivering in their coats.

Joseph turned to her. "If there's an emergency, you can go to the neighbors." He pointed to a house just becoming visible over a far hill.

Katie exited the car and turned to speak to Joseph. "Don't worry."

"I'll see you this evening!" Joseph turned in his seat and smiled at her. That flash of white was the last thing she saw before the car took off again and roared away.

She turned to the kinner. They stood huddled on the porch, four in a row, staring at her silently. "It's cold!" Caleb complained.

"Come inside, then," Katie replied, taking him by the hand.

***

Katie untied her cape and took stock of the house. It was big and plain and clean, mostly; the kitchen table was still covered with the remnants of what looked like a large and messy breakfast.

"Your daed told me that Hezekiah and Jeremy have their chores," Katie said, looking at the boys. "Will you be all right then?" she asked them.

"Yes, Mrs. Olsen." They looked at each other and bounded out of the front door.

"Emma, I'll help you clear up in the kitchen if you'll show me where everything is," Katie offered. Emma looked down and said nothing, but led the way to the big farmhouse kitchen.

The baby, Caleb, followed her, climbing up into a chair to watch her as she cleaned. His big blue eyes looked wistful.

Katie was very much aware of those blue eyes. She turned, smiled at Caleb, and finally said, "Don't you have chores to do, Caleb?"

"He's supposed to sweep the floors and take out the trash," Emma answered.

"I don't want to do them yet," Caleb informed her. "I want to watch Mrs. Olsen. Do you know any stories?" he asked, resting his chin on his hands.

Katie smiled as she wiped the table down. "Yes, I know a few stories that a little boy might like." She began to tell him some of the bedtime stories she had once told Peder - the story of the duck and the goose, the story of the little frog and the big frog, the story of the fox and the hen.

Caleb watched her all the while with those unblinking blue eyes, not moving, seeming hardly to breathe. He listened raptly and said nothing as she talked on and on.

When she finally ran out of stories, he said simply, "Mamm used to tell me stories all the time. I miss that."

Katie's hands froze in mid-air. She and Emma both stood stock-still, staring at him.

Caleb smiled and bounded away from the table and ran off to do chores with a five-year-old's heedlessness, but Katie stood motionless, blinking.

Emma closed a cabinet door a bit too quickly, and the slamming sound jolted Katie back to herself.

"Let's start," she said at last.

Katie soon discovered that Emma was a competent, budding homemaker, and would probably have been fine if she hadn't been burdened with all the housework. Katie observed that Emma tended to cook things too long, and was not yet a successful baker, but with more time and training, Katie reckoned she would make a fine cook.

"You're a good cook," she told her, smiling. Emma gave her a quick sideways look. "That's what Mamm always said," she said quietly, and then, after a long pause, "I miss her, too."

Between them, Katie and Emma made lunch and dinner, and got a start on the next day's breakfast. It was hard, hot work, done over a wood stove, but gradually the table filled up with fried potato pancakes with applesauce and sour cream, cornbread, biscuits, buttered noodles with ham and peas, fried chicken, lemon cookies, and bologna sandwiches with thick slices of homemade cheese for the boys.

The aroma of baking lured Caleb back from his sweeping. He had crawled up in a chair at the table, munching the cookie that Katie had not been able to deny him.

Katie was just putting a jug of tea on the table when Hezekiah and Jeremy came in from their work. Their bright eyes lit up.

"It smells so good in here!" Jeremy cried, inhaling. "Biscuits!"

"I'm starving. I could eat the whole plate." Hezekiah laughed, with a telling glance at the mound of biscuits Katie had just taken out of the oven.

"They're for dinner," Emma told him. "We made sandwiches for you."

The boys sat down and would have fallen directly on the bologna sandwiches, but Katie cleared her throat.

"Grace first," she reminded them.

The kinner clasped their hands obediently, and they prayed silently for a few moments. Then without further ado the boys annihilated the plate of bologna sandwiches, and also polished off the cheese straws, dried apples and pie that Katie piled on their plates.

"This is the first good meal we've had in four months! Wait 'til Daed gets back!" Jeremy blurted out.

Emma flushed as red as a beet, and Katie felt compelled to

come to her defense.

"It isn't easy to cook and wash and clean for five people every day," she reminded the boys. "Be grateful that your sister loves you enough to cook your meals."

The boys looked down and mumbled their apologies, and Emma shot Katie a look that had a flicker of gratitude in it.

CHAPTER EIGHT

When Joseph arrived at his home that evening, he could scarcely believe his eyes. Freshly washed laundry flapped from the clothesline. The heavenly scent of baking bread reached him even in the car. And off to one side of the house, he could see Katie weeding the kitchen garden with Caleb in tow.

He could feel his mouth dropping open slightly. It looked as if the newcomer was off to a flying start, and it was clear that at least one of his kinner had already approved her. Katie and Caleb were laughing and giggling together as if they'd always been friends.

Joseph's smile faded at the thought. A pang of something almost like resentment stabbed him, and then was gone. He put a hand over his eyes.

"Daed!"

Emma waved to him from the front porch. "Come and see

what we have for dinner!"

He smiled at her and said, "I will come back. But call Mrs. Olsen."

Katie arrived soon after, leading Caleb by the hand. A few tendrils of brown hair had escaped from her bonnet and trembled with her breath. She was flushed and laughing and looked happier than Joseph had ever seen her.

He stared at her in amazement. He hadn't noticed it before, but now he had to admit that Katie was a lovely girl. Joseph was stabbed by another fleeting emotion – an emotion that made him feel ashamed.

He spoke quickly, in an effort to banish it. "Are you ready to go home?"

"Yes," she replied, and climbed into the back seat.

Katie was still breathless and laughing as she sat down. She wiped her brow. "Whew! We had a busy day, but we got many things accomplished. You'll find dinner ready, and enough for breakfast tomorrow. Everyone had a good lunch. The clothes are washed and ironed, and we weeded the kitchen garden. We'll till it tomorrow, so it will be ready for planting when the new owners arrive."

"Thank you, Katie."

Joseph looked at her again, and again had the odd sensation that he was seeing her for the first time. Nothing had changed, except that she had been sad before, and now she looked happy.

Yet this small change made her look like a completely different woman.

It was surprising, and slightly discomforting. He adjusted one shoulder slightly. Still, it was plain that things were off to a good start, and the prospect of an orderly household was a great relief.

During the drive, Katie regaled him with the small stories of what had happened in his home while he was gone. Joseph, chafing under the enforced separation from his kinner, was hungry for these details.

When the car arrived at the Fisher farm, he thanked her again, and with genuine gratitude.

"I'm glad that things went well on your first day," he told her. "Is there anything you need, anything that would help you?"

Katie considered, and then shook her head. "I'm content," she smiled.

He looked at her and couldn't help resting his eyes on her face for a moment too long. Yes, she was content. It was amazing that a woman who had been so sad just days before could today look so happy. Her eyes were positively sparkling.

For the first time, Joseph noticed that they were green.

"I'll be back at the same time tomorrow," he smiled, and waved in farewell.

He watched her as she skipped up the porch steps and disappeared into the house.

But he was silent, and looked troubled, all during the long drive back.

Over the next few weeks, Joseph became increasingly accustomed to riding back and forth with Katie. She almost always seemed calm and happy, a change that continued to amaze him.

She laughed often, was a pleasant travel companion, and the news she gave him was always good; the kinner were busy and obedient, and projects that had gone undone were slowly being taken care of.

Family meals were always varied, delicious, and right on time. The laundry and dishes were sparkling. The kitchen garden had gone from a neglected weed patch to a neat brown rectangle filled with rich soil ready for planting. The yard was trimmed and neat, and the house was always clean and tidy.

But best of all, he could see for himself that, for the first time since Sarah's death, his kinner's lives were improving. His kinner seemed happier and more secure. Emma was finally beginning to relax. She no longer wore that strained, worried look that came from having too much work and too little time. She was smiling and giggling again, like a 12-year-old girl should.

Hezekiah, he suspected, was just a bit smitten by the pretty Katie and was trying to behave more like a man. Joseph smiled and shook his head. Jeremy was still a handful, but his manners had shown improvement since Katie had arrived.

And it was becoming plain that five-year-old Caleb adored Katie, and that the feeling was mutual.

It was good. And not good.

Joseph sighed.

***

Katie climbed into the back seat of the car, laughing from something that Jeremy had said in parting. The kinner crowded around the car window to say goodbye for the evening.

"All right, that's enough," Joseph told them mildly. "Let Katie go. She'll be back tomorrow."

As the car took off, Katie laughed a little. "I'm sorry, it's my fault. I just enjoy them so much."

Joseph said nothing. He was becoming curious about her, and wanted to ask questions. It would be bad manners to ask questions, especially of such a troubled past, but he couldn't resist encouraging her to talk.

"It's a shame we didn't meet earlier," he said. "Just a county over, too."

"Oh, I was gone these past five years," she said, still pleasantly, but her smiled faded. "I married and moved away to Ohio."

"Ah. Perhaps you met my cousins there – Silas and Hans Lapp?"

"Oh – oh, yes!" Katie cried, looking up suddenly. "I did meet them once, I think! The twins?"

"Yes. They are hard to miss. The tallest men in that county, and five counties round, I hear."

Katie laughed merrily, showing fine straight teeth and the hint of a dimple in one rosy cheek. To his horror, Joseph felt that dimple make his heart begin to race.

He turned around again, pretending to observe the sky, to keep her from reading the inappropriate thought in his face. "See! Bad weather is coming tomorrow," he said, pointing to a small dark line of clouds on the horizon.

Katie turned to look. "Yes, it is," she murmured, and fell silent. Joseph put it down to his awkward and abrupt change of subject.

But once she saw it, Katie's eyes stayed fixed on the small

but ominous omen for the rest of the drive home.

***

The next day, Joseph's prediction came true. The sky was dark, and the clouds were low and threatening. It looked like a spring storm was in the offing.

Joseph noticed that Katie was unusually quiet. He glanced back at her. She was looking out the car window at the clouds. Her eyes were dull and dark. Tiny wrinkles creased the corners of her mouth.

Without warning, the laughing, happy girl had vanished. To Joseph's surprise, the sad, somber woman he had first met had returned.

He was startled by how much the change distressed him. The charming, pretty girl he had come to know had suddenly been replaced by a listless, depressed stranger.

In his surprise, Joseph blurted out the question in his mind.

"Katie, is something wrong?"

She didn't reply immediately. Her dull eyes were fixed on some invisible point on the horizon. Joseph followed her gaze, thinking that he would see some sign of what had upset her, but there was nothing there but the fast-moving clouds.

"No...no, nothing's wrong."

Her voice, usually so light and happy, was flat and

toneless.

Joseph stared at her in concern. Perhaps something had happened to remind Katie of her grief. He felt a pang of compassion. She had been such a help to him; he had almost forgotten that she was mourning her own losses.

"If you're not feeling well, we can manage for a day or two," he told her kindly. "Take a rest, if you'd like."

Katie shook her head and said nothing. That silent gesture, so expressive of hopelessness, was more alarming to Joseph than if she had cried.

He said no more, but bit his lip, debating with himself. The kinner would be sure to notice that something was wrong – perhaps even barrage her with questions. He would have to get out ahead of it.

When they arrived at his house and Katie got out of the car and went inside, Joseph followed her. He didn't enter the house, but stood silently in the open doorway.

Katie was facing away from him, but Joseph saw Emma's head come up. He motioned to her silently.

She came outside, all curiosity.

"What is it, Daed?" she asked.

He lowered his voice. "Katie is a little sad today. She has had her own losses, remember. We must be considerate of her. Get her off to yourself today, if you can, so that the boys won't ask her awkward questions."

Emma nodded. "I will, Daed."

He kissed her brow. "That's my good girl."

But he stood watching at the door for a long moment after.

***

All that day, Joseph felt worried. Perhaps it was the weather – the sky threatened a downpour all day long, and the winds shook the four corners of the building where he worked making furniture. He was glad when the workday ended, and was eager to be home.

To his great relief, when he arrived, Katie looked much less somber. She came out of the house arm-in-arm with Emma, and Joseph silently blessed his daughter for her thoughtfulness.

But when she arrived in the car, he soon found that, once again, Katie had been the giver.

Her pretty eyes had regained some of their old sparkle. To his great surprise, she motioned him to join her in the back seat.

He stared at her in surprise, but got out of the car and joined her there.

"I wanted to tell you something in private," she whispered. "Something very important happened to Emma today. I know you would want me to tell you."

He inclined his ear, and Kate leaned in to whisper. Her breath was warm on his ear, and faintly fragrant.

His eyebrows arched up sharply. He turned quickly and looked questioningly at Katie. Katie smiled and nodded. Joseph felt his eyes pooling with quick tears. It didn't seem possible. How the time had run away!

"If only Sarah were here today," he whispered.

Without noticing, he reached out for Katie's hand and took it in his own. Her hand was warm and reassuring, and clasped his without pulling away.

Until he came to himself and withdrew his own hand – what seemed like much later.

CHAPTER NINE

The bad weather continued for days. Winter seemed to be waging one last battle against the advance of spring, and the sky was blue every night with sunsets like branching fire. The winds gusted and died, and gusted again. Heavy clouds scudded across the sky.

Katie lay awake in her narrow bed, unable to go to sleep. She passed a trembling hand over her shoulder. Her skin was smooth and fair now. The stain was all but gone.

Lightning suddenly turned the bedroom a lurid white, then faded, then flashed again. Katie closed her eyes. She hated the lowering sky and the thunder. Maybe it was a sign of God's judgment, of His anger. She was sure that her surgery – prompted by her pride and vanity – had been very wrong.

Then there was her most recent sin. She turned her face into the pillow. That thing she had begun to feel for Joseph Lapp. The thing she could barely admit to herself, much less to God. But she must admit it.

"Oh, Lord, forgive me," she began, but before she could get any farther, there was a shattering clap of thunder and a violent lightning strike. She almost shrieked aloud.

Our God is a consuming fire.

Katie pulled the quilt over her head like a child. Oh God, she prayed at last, Are you still angry? Can't I have one small moment of peace?

The howling wind outside her window was the only reply.

When she finally did drop off to sleep, the moaning of the wind invaded her dreams. Sometimes, she dreamt she heard Peder's voice crying in it.

The next morning, the weather took a turn for the worse. The wind shrieked at every window and moaned from the kitchen fireplace. The sound of a low, constant roar filled the trees outside, as rivers of air tossed them to and fro.

Katie stood on the front porch, shivering in her cape as the headlights of the sedan crested the hill and advanced through the dark. It was 5 am, but it was still black as midnight and raining heavily.

As soon as the car pulled to a stop, she scurried in.

"What weather!" Joseph exclaimed as she settled in. "Are you all right?"

Katie shook herself. "I got a little drenched. The rain is as cold as ice!"

"I heard that there may be storm winds today," Joseph said. "Maybe even a tornado."

Katie pulled her cape closer about her. "I'll keep the kinner inside."

"There is a root cellar underneath the kitchen floor," Joseph told her. "If there is danger, you can take the kinner there until it passes. Emma will show you where."

Katie fell silent. She didn't like the mental image at all, but was unable to banish it. The wind shook the little car as it moved, and at one point rocked it so fiercely that even the taciturn Mr. Shandy broke out with a startled expletive.

Joseph looked back at her and smiled reassuringly. But Katie was barely able to muster a nod in reply and did not feel reassured.

The light of dawn didn't do much to allay Katie's fears. The world gradually became lighter, though never really light. The sky remained a dark, sullen gray, and the wind whipped the trees.

When they arrived at the Lapp house, Joseph reached back suddenly and took her arm. Katie looked up in surprise.

"Are you going to be all right?" he asked.

Katie was astonished, even in her distress. His vivid eyes had an odd look – almost intense.

She stammered, "Yes, I think so. Don't worry." She tried

to smile, but felt her lips move crookedly. She opened the car door and rushed out through the rain.

She turned and watched the car disappear down the road. As it pulled away, she could still see Joseph's face turned toward her.

Emma was waiting for her just inside the door. "I'm glad you're here, Katie," Emma said softly. "I'm frightened."

Katie reached out and took Emma in her arms. They had become much closer in the last few months, and for her part, Katie almost thought of Emma as...

She interrupted herself, shutting out that line of thought.

"Where are the boys?" she asked.

"Caleb is still upstairs. Hezekiah and Jeremy are out in the barn, tending the animals."

The sound of the wind was clearly audible inside the house, and the gusts seemed to be picking up. Katie walked out onto the porch and looked up at the sky. The clouds were racing past, and the sky had taken on a sickly yellowish cast.

Katie ran out into the yard and out to the big red barn. The cows inside were lowing anxiously as Hezekiah and Jeremy worked.

Hezekiah looked up and saw her standing there.

"Hezekiah," she called, "you and Jeremy come inside. As

soon as you're finished here."

"We're almost done now," Jeremy called back.

Katie stood at the door until they had finished their work, and then led them back to the house. She threw her cape over her head, but the boys got drenched and arrived to the house shivering and wet.

"Go and change your clothes," she told them, "and then come down and dry out by the fireplace."

Thunder suddenly boomed and rumbled overhead, and there was a crack of lightning.

Caleb appeared from nowhere and ran to Katie, his big blue eyes like saucers. She picked him up and hugged him close. He was terrified. She could feel it.

"Let's sit down and have some breakfast, Caleb," she told him. "Would you like that?"

He nodded mutely, and she kissed his cheek. It was as firm and smooth as a ripe peach.

Katie set Caleb down at the table and tried to bury her anxiety by busying herself with breakfast. She cooked cornmeal mush, she peeled fruit, she made pancakes and fried eggs. The kitchen was soon warm and filled with the golden light from the wood burning stove, and many lamps.

But outside, the wind was blowing harder than ever. The kinner ate almost in silence; there was no laughter, no play.

Something small suddenly hit the roof. Then again, and again. Katie looked outside in dismay. Hail was falling everywhere, hailstones the size of walnuts.

"Emma, where is the root cellar?" Katie asked.

"In back of the pantry," Emma quavered.

"Show me."

Emma led her to a small closet pantry in the wall. There was a door in the back, and when she opened it, a stair led down into darkness.

A tearing and peeling sound from the roof made Katie turn and snatch Caleb up in her arms. "Everyone down to the cellar! Bring the lamps! Hurry!"

The kinner clambered down the steps, and the lamplight made the shadows jump and quaver. The walls were covered in shelves, and the shelves were filled with jars. There was just enough room for the five of them to sit on the floor together.

Katie set Caleb down and turned back to close the cellar door. At the top of the stairs, she had a clear, straight view to the front door. Through it she could see the low clouds swirling together into a narrow, twisting funnel.

"Oh, God, God help!" she cried, and slammed the cellar door. Her hands fumbled for a lock, but there was none.

By this time the ground had begun to tremble, and then

there was a sound that Katie would never forget – a deep, heavy rumble, like an oncoming train.

"Katie, Katie, I'm scared, I'm scared!" Caleb shrieked, and she stumbled down the steps to take him in her arms. She knelt down on the ground with the baby in her arms, gasping prayers. Emma was crying and clutching at Katie's skirt, and the boys were silent, but sitting rigid on the ground, their eyes wide and terrified.

Suddenly there was a flash and a deafening explosion outside. A wave of energy surged through the earth, through their bodies, and out again. Emma and Caleb screamed. Katie bent over, trying to shield Caleb with her body.

Katie heard herself crying. She was panting and praying silently, Oh, God, please, don't let me lose my family again. Please, please God!

There was a sound of crashing and splintering wood outside that suggested that something heavy was being demolished. The walls shook once again.

Then, just as suddenly, there was an eerie silence. The rumbling sound stopped. A small tinkling and a distant crash were the only sounds in a long 30 seconds of deep quiet.

Then the rumbling started again.

This time it was even more intense. The ground shook violently, and Katie could hear the sound of plates and jars smashing in the kitchen above. There was a heavy crash directly above them, as if a tall piece of furniture had slammed to the ground.

Emma shrieked and covered her ears. Hezekiah had thrown his arms around Jeremy, and Caleb was mute with terror. His fingers dug into Katie's arms like the claws of a terrified baby animal.

There was another loud bang, like a door slamming. Then bang again.

And then, suddenly, it was quiet.

They all crouched low on the floor, listening. The only sound for a long while was Emma's crying.

Katie held Caleb, straining her ears. Five minutes passed, ten. There was a vast, ominous silence from above.

Katie put her hand out and smoothed Emma's hair. "Is everyone all right?" she asked.

The boys nodded, silent. Emma shook her head, but Katie could see that she wasn't hurt. She looked down at Caleb. The terrified expression on his face pierced her heart.

She rocked him, made soothing hush sounds. "It's all right, my little man," she told him. "It's all right, it's all right." She smoothed her hand over his hair.

Hezekiah looked up at the cellar door. "Someone should go up and see what happened," he said.

Katie frowned. "I'll go. The rest of you, stay here."

She looked down at Caleb and reluctantly handed him over to Emma. He threw his arms around his sister's neck and clung there.

"Be careful, Katie," Emma whimpered.

"I will."

CHAPTER TEN

Katie stood up slowly and with difficulty. Her legs were trembling and felt as if they were made of straw. She grabbed the stair rail and climbed slowly.

She grasped the handle and pushed at the cellar door, but something was blocking it. Katie pushed again, and the door made a scraping sound as it gave way to reveal a scene of chaos.

The house was a shambles. The kitchen table had been knocked over, and all their breakfast plates and glasses were lying shattered on the floor. A chair had been thrown against the cellar door, and others were lying all over the living room. The front door was standing open and hanging from only one hinge.

She walked across the floor feeling oddly detached, as if none of it was real.

Katie walked outside, down the porch steps, and around

the side of the house. The clouds were breaking up, and she could even see blue sky in spots. There was no wind, not even a breeze.

Then Katie looked toward the barn.

To her horror, it was gone. The big red barn was gone. The cows, the milking equipment, the tractor – all gone.

She stumbled across the ground – the ground, because every tree, every plant, and even the grass had been sucked out and vacuumed up. The only clue that there had ever been a building there at all was a sprawling field of litter that started where the barn had been and trailed out all the way to the horizon.

Then Katie turned back to look at the house. To her amazement, the only structural damage it had sustained was a few lost roof tiles and a dangling front door.

Katie stared, and then dropped to her knees, trembling.

It was a miracle.

Something hard and dark suddenly broke open inside her, and for the first time in months, Katie could sense the presence of God. It flooded down on her like sunlight, like a comforting hand laid on her shoulder, like a warm embrace. Suddenly she knew, just knew, that God didn't hate her even for her foolishness. She knew that He loved her, had always loved her, even when she thought that He rejected and condemned her. Katie closed her eyes, weeping.

Oh, God. Oh, God, thank you, she prayed. She put a hand to her mouth. Thank you for my life. Thank you for the babies. We could all have been...

She hugged herself and started to cry. Oh, God, you're not angry. You don't hate me. You're not angry. You saved our lives! You're not angry, you're not angry.

Katie sobbed, and then laughed in pure, joyous relief. Something in her heart broke free and escaped to heaven as she lifted her hands.

Through her tears, Katie saw Mr. Shandy's car suddenly screech to a halt in front of the house. She saw Joseph jump out while it was still moving and take the porch steps at a single bound. His frantic voice boomed out from inside the house:

"Emma! Boys!"

And then the shrill calls of the kinner from below. The cacophony of their frantic reunion. Katie knelt on the ground with her eyes closed, listening to their voices.

Then, to her surprise, she heard the sound of a door slamming and feet on the porch.

"Katie!"

She opened her eyes. Joseph was standing on the edge of the porch, searching with his eyes.

And then he was beside her. Just that quickly.

If the tornado had snatched her up from the ground, it couldn't have done a better job than Joseph Lapp. One instant, Katie was spinning over the ground, and then she was folded in Joseph's arms. One brown hand cradled her head, and the other clasped her waist.

"Oh, my love," he murmured, and then his lips were on hers. Katie closed her eyes and yielded joyously. She twined her hands around Joseph's broad back as he spun her again, laughing and crying at the same time.

He pressed his lips against her cheek. "I thought I'd lost you," he was saying. "But I can't lose you, Katie. I know it's still very soon to ask. But stay with me."

He pulled back, and looked down at her with pleading blue eyes. "I've come to love you these past months. Tell me that you love me," he whispered.

And he kissed her again, this time in a way that even Erik had never done. Katie gasped in surprise, and her fingers curled into his back.

"I love you, Joseph Lapp," she confessed. "And I will stay with you."

Over Joseph's broad shoulders, she could see the kinner standing on the porch. Emma was smiling, the boys were bug-eyed, and Caleb shouted, "Can Mrs. Olsen move in and be our mamm at night, too?"

Joseph smiled down at her with his bright blue eyes.

"Especially at night," he agreed, and the sound of his laughter made little prickles go up and down Katie's back.

He knelt down on one knee and took her hand. "Katie, may I court with you?" he asked.

Katie felt quick tears spring to her eyes again. She was unable to speak, and so she only nodded.

***

Later that evening Katie and Joseph walked arm in arm in the purple twilight. Crickets had begun to chirp softly here and there, a sign that spring had truly arrived. From where they stood, the soft lights of the house glowed yellow, and the sound of the kinner's laughter floated over the fields.

"I need to tell you something, Katie," Joseph confessed. "I still miss Sarah," he murmured, looking out to the horizon. "I still hurt. I never expected to fall in love again, and never expected it to happen so soon." He took a tendril of her hair and tucked it tenderly behind her ear. "Is it all right? Do you understand?"

Katie looked down and nodded. "I understand. I miss Erik, too. I miss…." She broke off, swallowed. She still couldn't say the words: I miss Peder.

Joseph pulled her close and held her. She rested her head on his shoulder.

"Maybe it will never go away, the grief," she said softly.

"Maybe it isn't supposed to, Joseph. Can we forget those we loved? Should we?" She turned and cupped his face in her hand. "No. We love again, but we should not forget."

Joseph took her hand and kissed it. They stood together, watching as the purple twilight deepened, and the first star of evening appeared.

"I wanted to sell this farm," Joseph said at last, "but now I'll rebuild it. You will come to live here, Katie, and this house will bloom like a rose in spring. It will be a sad place no more."

He looked down at her and she could feel rather than see him smile. "You have showed us the way home."

She smiled in return, but shook her head. "No, Joseph. Not I. That was Someone else."

END OF BOOK 1.

Thank you for Reading!

I hope you enjoyed reading this as much as I loved writing it! If so, there is a sample of the next book in the next chapter. You can find the whole book in eBook and Paperback format at your favorite online book distributors.

All the best,

Ruth

LANCASTER COUNTY SECOND CHANCES – BOOK 2

CHAPTER ONE

Katie slid into the back seat of Eli Shandy's car. As the Lapp house receded into the background, Joseph reached out with one large brown hand and pulled her to his side. Katie snuggled deep into his arms with a sigh.

She was still caring for Joseph's children, and the two of them were still observing the proprieties that demanded that Amish singles – even engaged ones -- must not be alone together.

Although, Katie had to admit, their adherence to these rules were becoming looser and more tenuous by the day. She could hardly wait for the wedding so she could kiss Joseph freely and openly.

Not that they weren't kissing anyway. There seemed to be an unspoken agreement between Joseph and their driver, because Eli Shandy was even more blind and deaf now than at first – which is to say, extremely. Even when Katie dared to train her eyes on Joseph's lips, and he took the hint, and they spent the next five minutes exploring the general subject of lips and a few other things besides. Mr. Shandy never so much as cast a glance in the rearview.

Even so, Katie found herself wishing their driver at Jericho -- and feeling guilty for it.

"It's terrible to be *almost* married," she whispered in Joseph's ear.

Joseph smiled and pressed her close. "Only a little while longer," he replied.

"Two more *months*," she grumbled.

Joseph leaned in and blew in her ear, and she pinched him, and they made such a moving and shaking in that little car that Mr. Shandy could hardly have failed to notice if he *had* been blind and deaf. But he said nothing, and took no notice, until the car pulled up to the front door of the Fisher farm.

"Kiss me, Joseph!" she whispered, and he kissed her again before the sound of the front door opening meant that she had to pull away.

Katie's little sister Bett was standing on the front porch, wiping her hands on her apron. "Why, Katie, what happened to your hair?" she asked innocently.

Katie felt her cheeks going hot. She put up her hand and hastily smoothed the unruly tendrils. She looked back at the car to see a flash of white against brown: Joseph grinning at her from the car window.

"Never mind."

Katie passed through the kitchen on the way to the stairs and caught a glimpse of her mother and half a dozen other women sewing in the living room. Mary Fisher waved her hand and made a shooing gesture that she usually reserved for her geese.

"Go away, Katie!" she laughed. "You can't see your quilt until your wedding day!"

The other women giggled as Katie smiled and mounted the stairs to her own bedroom.

She closed the door behind her, walked to the window, and took off her bonnet. Far in the distance, she could see the road to the Lapp farm and just on the horizon, the glint of Eli Shandy's car as it crested the last hill and disappeared from sight.

She plopped down on her bed, smiling. The change in her life had been nothing short of a miracle. It was true that she still had nights where Erik reached for her from the shadows, or worse, when Peder's sweet voice pierced her dreams and made her sit up, wide-eyed, in the dark.

But those nights would have come anyway, and soon she would have Joseph's arms to comfort her. She would wake to the sweet sound of Caleb's voice, and the voices of the other children. She already thought of them as hers.

And there might even be more children to come, hers and Joseph's together, to heal their hearts and bring them new joys.

Katie hugged her pillow to her body happily, and gratitude welled up in her like a clear spring. Eventually it spilled into a glad prayer, a prayer of thanksgiving.

Thank You, Lord, Katie prayed, *You have given me so much! Thank you most of all for showing me how wrong I was to fear You. For showing me that you love me in all the ways I know and understand.*

That night at dinner, Katie's family was more glad and talkative than usual. John Fisher's brown eyes glowed when they rested on Katie, but they were also sometimes over-bright. He blew his nose into a large red handkerchief once or twice, and his wife smiled a bit ruefully and put her hand on his arm.

After dinner, he went out to the porch and sat down in the swing to watch night fall over his fields. They were full and high with corn, and the evening air was fragrant with sweet grasses and near-ripeness.

Katie sat down beside him and put her head on his shoulder. "I will still miss this, Daed," she said quietly.

Her father gazed out over his fields. "You can always sit and talk to me, Katze," he said, and then coughed. "That never changes."

He fell silent, and then asked: "You are sure, then?"

She lifted her head and looked at him in astonishment. "Why, what do you mean?"

"It just seemed... very soon to me...

Thank you for Reading!

91

I hope you enjoyed reading this as much as I loved writing it! If so, you can find the rest of the book in eBook and Paperback format at your favorite online book distributors.

All the best,

Ruth

ABOUT THE AUTHOR

Ruth Price is a Pennsylvania native and devoted mother of four. After her youngest set off for college, she decided it was time to pursue her childhood dream to become a fiction writer. Drawing inspiration from her faith, her husband and love of her life Harold, and deep interest in Amish culture that stemmed from a childhood summer spent with her family on a Lancaster farm, Ruth began to pen the stories that had always jabbered away in her mind. Ruth believes that art at its best channels a higher good, and while she doesn't always reach that ideal, she hopes that her readers are entertained and inspired by her stories.

29216589R00059

Made in the USA
San Bernardino, CA
16 January 2016